CRYPTID CAROLS

TO SING IN THE DARK

CRYPTID CAROLS

TO SING IN THE

DARK

Published by MEMENTO VIVERE PRESS
www.mementoviverepress.com
First Edition, October 2024

Publisher and Illustrator, Ynes Freeman
ynes@mementoviverepress.com

Editor-in-Chief and Formatter, Leo Otherland
leo@mementoviverepress.com

Cover design by Rue Sparks
www.ruesparks.com

Print ISBN: 978-1-964501-02-4
Ebook ISBN: 978-1-964501-03-1

For all the quirky lurkers.
Keep it weird.

CONTENTS

OH, CHRISTMAS LÄMP

by A.P. Hawkins

Oh, Christmas LÄmP
Oh, Christmas LÄmP
How colorful your twinkling!

In winter dark, young moths do sleep
Cold freezes, bites, and tears their wings.
I should join their hibernation,
Let frost have its domination!

But now I find I cannot rest.
For something wild stirs in my breast!
I hum a carol as I fly
Toward lights that twinkle in the night.

The people string them everywhere,
O'er roof and hearth and piney tree.
Unwary Mothman to ensnare,
By love of lights a-glittering.

The Mothman sees the pretty lights
Cannot resist the twinkles bright
Oh, Christmas LÄmP
Oh, Christmas LÄmP
How colorful your twinkling!

More plentiful than fireflies,
Bejeweled beacons in the night.
I fly in close, reach out so bold
To touch, possess, dear LÄmP to hold.

Could I resist a thing so grand?
Tugging my heart by a strand.
I hum a carol in the snow
And how my love for LÄmP does grow!

But in LÄmP's light hide unseen wires
Like spider webs 'round heart's desire.
I pay no heed to tangling line,
Eyes dazzled by this LÄmP of mine.

> *So he is drawn, Mothman to flame*
> *The siren song of LÄmP to blame*
> *Oh, Christmas LÄmP*
> *Oh, Christmas LÄmP*
> *How colorful your twinkl—**ZAP**!*

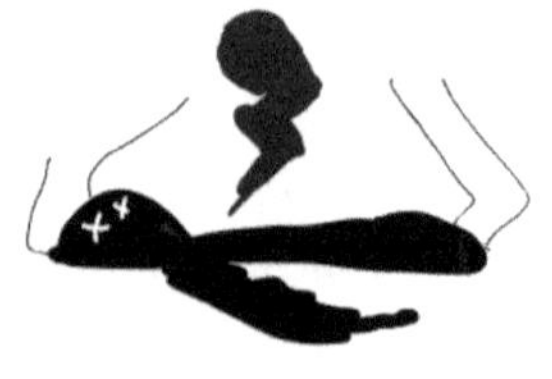

WINTER BALL

by Anna Guennadievna

On a dreary winter's night
Witte Wieven do take flight
Up the hill, into the starry night
No concern for Jack Frost's bite
Up the hill, like in previous age
Like pictures stepping off a page
Up the hill, for Christmas Eve
For a revel full of joie de vivre
White Women from a modern mould
Their dances all are grand and bold
No flards[1] of mist
No sausage and beer
But LED lights and a disco sphere
Under the shimmering Christmas moon
They will make merry until noon

[1] shred, a long, narrow strip that has been torn or cut off

THE DJINN AT SATURNALIA

by Angélique Jamail

The restless djinn had wandered currents of air and fire
to find solace, cryptid comforts, the locus of a djinn's
      desire.

Beyond sand dunes and glass palaces fused from crystal
      grit and flame,
he swept constellated skies in search of comfortable
      desire.

A symptom of malaise: bored with unchanging tahini,
      feta, lamb set to roast,
he sought new spices, flavors, the unexpected unfolding
      to quench his desire.

Also weary with use, the djinn renounced his demesnes;
      he abandoned burning
requests hurtled from all corners, grasped the chance to
      consider his own desire.

Jaded by mundane wishes, a narrow rotation of the same
      earthly needs, the djinn
flirted with smashing his powers, casting aside the
      shackle of every small, human desire.

Hiding his pangs, he convinced his friend to
      roam with him, an ifrit
bound to the djinn by debt, command,
      spark, purpose, desire.

They soared across the winedark sea, hazarding danger
        to flame
with tidal quenching whitecaps tipped in watery desire.

Slipped between slits in the movements of the sun,
they chased merry lilts, wine and ambrosia, the goblin-
        fruits of desire.

Into a round salon, all silk and cushions and camaraderie,
        they burned
out their journey, landing in the generous laps of
        unfettered desire.

What a calling of the solstice this was, the party lit with
        candles,
nectar dripping from fountains, sweets and meats for
        every known desire!

The ifrit asked the djinn, *What fancy steeped
        in burning
urgency does this gathering fulfill, what need of
        yours, what desire?*

He considered the question, then sank into a svelte
        couch, immolating
himself near revelers clad in lush laurels, floribundas,
        ranunculus of desire.

Such grand company! Libertine, freer than the wind over
        the dune sea. Flames
in every corner illuminated every fold of his heart. He
        thrilled to culinary desire.

The ifrit pruned a fat cluster of grapes from a bowl,
        roasted them with a scorching
touch, dangled them above the djinn's mouth, watched

him reach to sate his desire.

Tell me why we're here, the ifrit demanded. The
        djinn pulled the fire sprite
closer, plucked the heated grapes, burst them
        between his teeth, felt desire.

To be lost among this crowd, unnoticed, unbothered—
        to defy their flame-
drenched spirits—to not be feared or summoned—only
        this was the djinn's desire.

A holiday? Too banal a response. They surveyed the
        merry tableau: candlelit
lovers, shifting identities; the willing suspension of
        limitations; gifts exchanged; desire.

And everywhere, the festivities—indulgence—belied
        each reveler's desperate, burning
hope: for darkness to be consumed, for these long nights
        to melt. A simple desire.

Here, a djinn could be of use, on his own terms. He
        grasped the ifrit's warm
hand, pulled his companion close, breathed flames of
        longing, of purpose, of desire.

And when the rosy-fingered dawn finally, slowly, crept
        over the horizon, lighting
the world, the salon, the djinn and ifrit burned, reveling,
        illuminating every desire.

Once more, darkness was consumed, the festival
        completed. All sated. Every banked fire
quenched. And a scribe, Angeliqi Sacre, lounged in a
        corner, weaving the djinn's desire.

FOOTPRINTS

by Sarah Tollok

They fear what they
can't grasp the entirety of.

They fear us
because they only ever catch
a fleeting glimpse
or
find a tuft of soft, thick fur
or
a few LARGE footprints.

Here's the secret:
They can't catch us
because we only ever leave
a few footprints
in their world
before we *s h i f t* to another
and **settle**
and leave new footprints.

The veil between
one reality
and the next
(and the next and the next and the . . .)
is soft.

If you know how
to step gently
to dance gracefully
to humbly reach

and never doubt
that your next step
will land
someplace the same
yet someplace different.

But this isn't a story about us—
This is a story of the little-footed ones
whose steps spread far
in lines
in one time
in one place
in one rigid time/place understanding.

There is a night
—the longest night—
when the winds sweep away
our footprints even faster.

The little-footed gather
around hearths
and lanterns
and candles.
They share warmth
cheer
good food
and stories.

But in that long night
—the longest night—
some look deep into the flames
and they feel the darkness beyond
and they reach.

They R E A C H!

We feel it
and we draw closer
in solidarity
in excitement.

We are careless
and leave bold footprints
across clearings
through gates
near enough to chilled windows
to cloud them with our breath.

Do they see the shimmer?
Do they feel how close they are
to the *s h i f t?*
The veil is ready to part for them
with a sigh
with a single step.

But the glow
of the same lights
they lit
to ward off
the longest dark
draws them back in.

So, they settle where they are
by their own hearth
wrapped in a tattered quilt
and they reach instead
for the hand of a loved one
or to stroke the head
of a sleepy dog.

And so
we turn away

back to our own wanderings
only a few footprints
at a time.

But we want them to know,
the little-footed ones,
if ever they choose
to reach
to step boldly
and yet softly
they are welcome
to walk with us.

A Ballade of Kelpie & Pegasi

by Rue Sparks

As solstice sun thaws snow to sea
Springs and streams turn brined and bitter
The brackish foam swirls filigree
And Kelpies play where tide meets river
When bridges break and rivers rise
They haunt the bank as Townsfolk flee
Their hinds a grave and cold demise
Held fast to backs they can't break free

River and sea are wont to change
Water and waves make willful hearts
Some creatures cannot be made tame
And souls of longing tear apart
An Other, gray with snowy mane
With eyes that linger on open air
Whispers of life not water or rain
Of phantom wings and dreams elsewhere

While brethren haunt wild waterways
Minds full of mischief and misdeeds
The Other wanders, and idly strays
Lingers aside cattails and reeds
Shifts and dallies as stallion or mare
A human, man, woman or youth
Whichever shape or body they wear
Their skin never feels like their truth

Alone, seasons and floods pass by
The Other roams far from the waves

Haunts mills and coves, streams low and high
No places or names what they crave
One night ice creeps on the riverside
The wind carries yearning in song
Verse and melody like swelling tide
Voice beautiful, bitter and wrong

A Rusalka, hair free and coarse
Watches and sings as The Other arrives
Her song never stops, harsh and hoarse
Spins jaded tales of heartbroken lives
The Other awaits, but the end never comes
Twisting, a snake eating its tail
The only shift like the swell of a drum
No revenge or pride to unveil

"Why sing a song that has no end?"
The Other questions the weary spirit
"Some suffering can never mend;"
"Even without words I hear it."
"What pains you so deeply?" The Other asked.
"Why not move on and love anew?"
"Love and pain are not to be sundered,"
"Just like that which lives inside you."

Words dangled on The Other's tongue
They wrangled them through lips and teeth
Agony never breathed nor sung
"My skin is not what is beneath;"
"There is naught that sways the hunger."
"I've found no name nor means to cease;"
"I can no sooner harness thunder,"
"Or barricade the storm's release."

"We suffer to love," The Rusalka hums.
"But not all suffering is bound."

"What will you give when the time comes?"
"If escape from your form is found?"
The Other remembers mischief and misdeeds
Of estuaries, tempests, the tide
No storm, no downpour tames the need
To free the shape and voice inside

The Rusalka's song lifted up,
Run betwixt trees, streams, and flowers
"Tread the mountain and cliffside up,"
"To where Mount Olympyus towers."
"Made of hooves, manes, feathers and fur,"
"Poseidon the sea-god their sire."
"They carry the god-king's thunder:"
"The Pegasi, your soul's desire."

"In the tracks from their hooves flow springs:"
"Untamable, stubborn, but free."
"I know not how to become one,"
"If outward change is meant to be,"
"But now I know to what I aim."
The Other's heart flutters and sighs,
"To tame a thing it needs a name,"
"And next is to see with my eyes."

Rusalka had cautioned their quest,
"Mayhaps t'will be too much to bear;"
"Even if you ascend the crest,"
"Will stagnance leave you in despair?"
Her words echo off shale and sod
The air thins the higher they climb
"Is pain beyond even a god?"
"What succor is for me to find?"

The thought grips their heart, cold and raw
But as winds cut the stone and the skies

With every step scales dry and thaw
Fins unfurl for fur to arise
Sharp edges of hooves round and trim
Gills grow into lungs light and full
From their tracks water fills to the brim
Breathes static from the lightning's pull

Coming upon the mountain's edge
A vast empty sky sprawls ahead
Clouds play with stars beyond the ledge
Olympus, where only gods tread
Closer than ever, yet eons away
Longing chokes new lungs in its grip
Lightning strokes along the wall's way
And Pegasi along their wing tip

At the sight, the longing bubbles
Burst through fractures in split facade
A barrier breached, a dam buckles
Changed when scales, fins, and gills dethawed
Quill, plume, muscle, and bone
Break through like reaching hands
Wings like lost limbs, but now their own
Awake from sleep with feathered strands

Limbs regained from coiled traps
Their wings compose a winding hymn
Push air beneath with mighty flaps
Hooves lift from rock on the cliff's brim
They swing forward off sky-touched bluff
Laughter and thermals echo afar
Blustery skies and clouds of fluff
The Other became what They Are

And though sometimes the story tells
Of a Kelpie That Would Not Be

That found their grave 'neath ocean swells
The Ones Who Know tell differently
Fed from no river, storm, or stream
A spring bloomed from the mountainside
The rebirth from an open-caged dream
When Pegasi breathed and Kelpie died

A Winter Night's Omen

by Sianyn Leigh

In the ides of December,
In the grip of mid-winter.
Before the Yuletide gladness
We observe sacred Mothmas.
For on this silent night
Mothman does take flight.
Harbinger and omen,
Portent of Doom;
His dark shadow
O'er the holidays looms.

All the children are told
Not to be so bold
As to go out on Mothmas Night.
He'll give you such a fright
And lay down a harsh curse.
You'll never find worse
Than what suffers a town
That lets the great Mothman down.

As he flies o'verhead
You'd best be in your bed.
For if one soul he spies,
The season's cheer dies.
For surely tragedy will befall
The whole town, one and all.
But if none suffer his gaze
For another year we are safe.
So the prophecy does foretell

Of the Mothmas origin tale.

But one cold December
I did not remember,
And ventured into the night.
Soon, he I came upon
Skimming over a frozen pond—
The dreaded Mothman. On ice.

With skates laced over his claws
And red mittens on his paws,
He glided graceful and fair;
I had to stop and stare!
How I envisioned a harbinger to be
Bore no relation to what I did see.
For who could have predicted
An ice-skating cryptid?

Mothman wings spread,
Leg stretched in Arabesque,
The horror of it quickly dawned
What my walk had just spawned.
Oh, my mom would make such a fuss
I hadn't honored sacred Mothmas
And whatever doom now would come
Was all because of something I'd done!

Would the wells all run dry
Or the crops would all die?
Maybe the bridge would collapse,
Or all the telephone poles snap!
Whatever it was, I'm to blame—
A curse be upon my name!

Yet I still had half a chance
To avoid a dread happenstance.

For he hadn't yet seen me,
And if I was *really sneaky*,
Maybe I could slip back home
Before my presence is known.

Then he executed a perfect Axel
That my fear turned to dazzle.
My heartfelt gleeful cheer
Drew his baleful leer.
It froze me still as a stock
as he skidded to a stop.
We stared at one another
And the words I did mutter
That had my mother by chance hear—
The consequence I did shudder!
And I waited with heavy gloom
For the Omen to yell, "Doom!"
But he only stared in surprise
With red, burning eyes,
A harbinger in limbo
With me, likewise akimbo.
Both of us caught in the act—
Neither sure how to react.

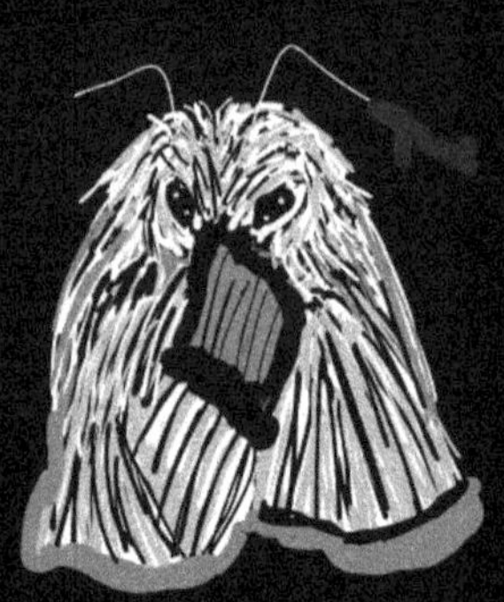

I gave a slight wave
And he whispered, "Behave—"
With one mittened claw
Pressed to his maw
In a sign to keep mum.
With a pivot and a twirl
Back to the ice he did whirl.
So, through the snow I fled
Straight back to my bed.

The night carried on
And nothing went wrong.

I never told a soul
What I saw on my stroll,
Never to venture out again
On a Mothmas evening,
Though I remembered all my life
The night I saw Mothman on ice.

EVENTIDE

by NJ Sullivan

Eventide on St. Nicholas Eve,
I hosted a well-appointed gathering.
Food and drink and merry tidings,
Family, mainly, but also friends joined the fray.

Conversation turned, as it so often
does, to matters of social import,
And the voices became less merry
and more angry in their tone.
And so I took my leave of them to
walk amongst the trees.
The only peace that I could find
was to walk amongst the trees.

In the forest's silence, I let my mind wander,
For I knew its paths quite well.
And the trail, though snow-covered,
Was clear between the trees.

A noise in the distance roused me from meditation;
The snap seemed to echo through the wood.
And my mind was drawn back to where I was standing,
Half a mile from Pigman Road.

They say the Pigman was a butcher,
Who lived here long ago.
To advertise his services,
He put a pig's head on a spike near the road.

An unpleasant man exiled by the townsfolk,
It's said one day he lost his mind,
And donned the face of a pig himself,
To right what he perceived were wrongs.

By the time he had burned through his rage,
Twenty seven heads lined his drive.
Twenty six of his ungrateful neighbors,
And one ungrateful pig.

The town took its vengeance,
And sent him to the Devil.
And burned and bulldozed his home,
To wipe out any memory of his horrible deed.

As I turned toward home,
I recalled another part of this gruesome fairy tale.
The locals will all tell you:
He'd been seen many times since then.

As the light faded and I made my way home,
I could sense something behind me.
I turned, and thought I saw something,
But my eyes in the darkness could not discern.

I continued on, hoping beyond hope,
That my feeling was a phantasm.
Simply a product of imagination in the dark.
But the feeling would not leave me, and so I turned
again.

There he stood.
A huge and looming shadow.
His head that of a massive pig's.
A gift from the Devil.

He wore a leather apron.
A massive cleaver in his hand.
Astride the woodland trail,
Steam rising from his form.

I turned and ran,
My only hope the warmth of home.
Back amongst my friends and family,
The loved ones I had spurned before.

But his stride was longer,
His stamina demonic.
Before I made a hundred yards,
His cleaver was at my neck.

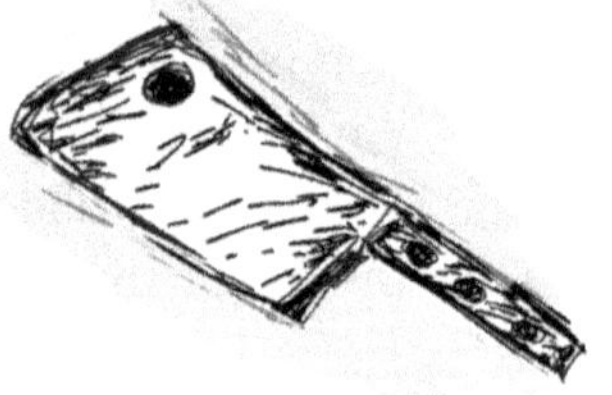

The sun rises on St. Nicholas Day,
And shines upon my face.
But not at home, not safe in bed,
On a spike at the roadside rests my head.

Nan Fenèt La
(Eyes in the Window)

by KT Seto

Gather round now you with hearts unafraid,
Hear the tale of why the Fànal must be made.
Ring the bells and look out for that fool, Tonton Nwèl.
But his eyes are not there staring in here at you.
The eyes in the windows are not those of friends;
The eyes that you see call you out to your end.

Ah mizé! Ah mizé!
Lift your voice now as one.
Chanté yon chanté for Réveillon.
Light the lamps and dance with joined arms.
Chanté ak danse, chanté ansanm!
Pretty house for the lost to protect petit uns.
Limen Fànal la, to protect everyone.

Desan ane and two score, give back five,
Is the number of years from that day to mine.
When they held the beast captive and barred from her
shields.
Made to toil at hard labor to pull cane from the fields,
Then into Bwa Kayiman she rushed to the dance,
And pledged death or vengeance if given the chance.
Ho man at the crossroads—Ezili Dantò too.
Sweet mother of love, she did beseech you
Limen Fànal la! She cried as she ran.
With the blood of that pig all over her hands.

Kiss the conch and cry freedom, she screamed with the rest.
But a bum full of powder was what the worst get.
And as she lay dying, she said she no go.
So, the Mambo switched hands, and she stopped the blood flow.
"Now you howl and you eat them. Get your fill with no rest."
Said the Mambo while painting the bones on her chest.
And she rose as a beast and rejoined the quest.

Down from the mountain, out to the sea,
She wanders the nights on her quest to break free.
But that war be long over and still she not done.
Her chalice of vengeance full of salt-water scum.
Je nan—the eyes, she catch yours with her dread
Ah mizé, she catch you. You know you be dead.

Ah mizé! Ah mizé!
Hold it high, your Fànal; lead the beast far away.
To the realm of the lwa where death she holds sway.

Hear her voice in the wind as she sings your last song,
Of a family betrayed, and a life gone far wrong.
Nails caked with blood and feet mired in mud,
Gleaming coils turned to a mane of matted dry fur.
Screams of despair morphed into howls,
Grunts of deep pain turned into growls.
Shoulders hunched to take blows, magnified to a bow.
Eyes filled with horror that ooze pus and glow.
And always she whispers her lament of pain.
"Bring me back me poor children, the ones who remain."

Her chanté, it's sadness, full of grief burned in souls.
Of love sold and broken, of life spoiled and sold.
Of death in the leaves, in the smoke, in the sand.
Of howls of rage swallowed and burned on with a brand.
Sweet tar stains her fingers like the blood on her claws,
Sweet death in the of drool dripping fresh from her jaws.
She waits in the shadows. "Call my name out," she howls.
But names they have power, so don't call them aloud.
Nou konnen who she was et konnen what she now.

Ah mizé! Loup Garou!
Hold it high, your Fànal; lead the beast far away.
To the realm of the lwa, where death she holds sway.

So, we learn. Cause the work, it not be yet done.
Fey Mama, we entreat thee, chanté ansanm
At the vigil, we chanté, chanté byen.
For we remember the why and have pity for them.
Like in her house waiting, our children they sleep.
But monsters have no homes, so that's why she weeps.
A mouth full of copper and eyes full of dust:
The flames cannot touch her. Her calling is just.
So we lead her away, broken beast past its day.
Lead her back to the crossroads, where the Papa holds
sway.

Ah mizé! Ah mizé! Hold it high, your Fànal.
Like her home made of light, but the size of a doll.
Shaggy beast made of teeth and painted with bones.
In the light of the moon, move away from our homes.

Ah mizé! Ah mizé!
Our tale is now done.
Chanté yon chanté for Réveillon.
Light the lamps and dance with joined arms.
Chanté ak danse, chanté ansanm.
Pretty house for the lost to protect petit uns.
Limen Fànal la, to protect everyone.

GLOSSARY

This work is in a melding of American AAVE English and Haitian Creole. As such, the grammar rules follow the melding of French/Latin standard with West African dialectics.

BWA KAYIMAN—Alligator Forest. Fun history tidbit: this was where the ceremony/meeting took place that marked the start of the Haitian revolution. A forest high in the mountains where the Marrons and the Indigenous tribes of Ayiti lived/hid from the French. At the ceremony, a Hougan and a Mambo (probably more than one of each) ended their meeting with a ceremony where they killed a black pig and used the blood to consecrate their work.

CHANTé—Sing.

CHANTé AK DANSE. CHANTé ANSANM—Sing and dance, sing together.

CHANTE BYEN—Sing good.

CHANTé YON CHANTé—Sing a song.

DESAN ANE AND TWO SCORE. GIVE BACK FIVE—233 years.

ET KONNEN—And know.

ÈZILI DANTò—Dual-natured lwa of love and death.

FàNAL—Gaily decorated lanterns shaped like little houses that are lit and carried on the path coming home from Christmas Eve services and placed on the window ledges and porches of houses. They stay lit all night during Réveillon.

FEY MAMA—Green mother.

HO MAN—A reference to Papa Legba, guardian of the doorway to the spirit land.

JE NAN—The eyes.

LIMEN FàNAL LA—Light the Fànal.

LWA—Also known as loa, they are considered to be the intermediaries between humans and the divine, or Bondye, and are believed to help people in their daily lives.

MIZé—Misery. Specifically, the Haitian concept of unending suffering, which they have had since the war for independence and the subsequent 100 years of reparations they paid to France for their freedom.

NOU KONNEN—We know.

PETIT UNS—Little ones.

RéVEILLON—All-night family feast that starts just after Christmas Eve services and lasts until sunrise. Children go to bed after placing their lanterns and shoes out for Tonton Nwél.

TONTON NWèL—The Haitian equivalent of Santa Claus.

IT WATCHES

by Alex Bauer

The beast arrives on nightfall's heels:
in dark, in smoke, in flame.
Logs spit sparks as fire consumes,
and all the while, it watches.

Snow sizzles in its cloudy breath,
or maybe on its tongue.
The oxen low in the nearby barn,
and from the dark, it watches.

Moonlight paints the pines above,
silver smeared on black.
Shadows dance beyond the glow,
and all the while, it watches.

Your hair stands up in angry wind,
its keen a mournful howl.
The loggers gather 'round the fire,
and in the night, it watches.

You ask to say a few kind words:
Prayer or praise or passion.
"A good ol' boy," the first man says,
and all the while, it watches.

Its eyes burn red amidst the dark,
with raw and righteous rage.
"Could've used him," your father scoffs,
and beyond the fire, it watches.

You shift your feet upon the ground,
snowmelt seeping in.
"We'll find one more," a faller adds,
and from the dark, it watches.

The ox dropped dead under the yoke,
A poor and wretched thing.
"He had kind eyes," you think to say,
and all the while, it watches.

"You're sentimental," Cook rumbles,
"but kinder than the rest."
You think it's slipped between the trees,
but still, you feel it watching.

A logging camp's no place for crying,
but sniffle still you must.
You burst with fear, "I saw it come!"
And though they laugh, it watches.

Its fearsome teeth and blood-red maw
can tear a man apart.
It's brought about because of death,
and you tell the camp, "It watches."

A Hodag now, dead oxen then—
it comes about through suffering.
You burn a corpse this Christmas night,
and tramping near, it watches.

"You shouldn't tell such awful tales."
Your father clouts you soundly.
With stinging cheek and bloodied lip,
you whisper soft, "I'm watching."

You hold your breath and wring your hands,
the creature drawing closer.
The men all laugh and poke their fun,
and from the dark, it pounces.

Fire flies in all directions;
you narrowly avoid it.
The Hodag roars its bestial rage,
and with a yell, you meet it.

With arms up high and mouth agape,
you walk toward the beast.
It rakes its claws amidst the coals,
and though it snarls, it watches.

"There's danger here," you plead aloud,
"and not all cheered his death.
Go find another camp to haunt,
and know I'll keep an eye out.

"For on this night—this holy night—
I make to you a promise:
When I am here, no deaths in vain."
Your arms fall down; it watches.

Its eyes are wary, its tail a club
that cracks the pyre asunder.
And in the smoke, you see . . . an ox?
And then you watch it vanish.

The Hodag snorts and rolls its head,
a shiver running through it.
It holds your gaze and steps toward you;
now all the camp is staring.

With huffing breath and dripping teeth,
it tips its face to yours.
You feel its might, its pain, its sorrow, and
you know now why it's watching.

From ox to ash to Hodag born,
its memory steeps in hurt.
The whip, the chain, the heavy yoke:
an animal, a victim.

"Never again while I'm still here,"
you tell the mighty beast.
The crowd is restless all around,
And you can feel them listening.

The Hodag slinks back through the fire,
and then into the forest.
Your heart beats fast and breath comes short;
yet still, you hope it watches.

You scold your father—a Christmas treat—
"Make sure you treat them kindly.
The Hodag's out there, filled with fight,
and you know it will be watching.

"No oxen whipped and driven dead;
no hurting horses, either.
I'll do my job and let you lead,
but know I'm always watching."

He nods and bows his wind-whipped head,
chastened and afraid.
"I'll see it done," he tells the ground,
and all the men start nodding.

And from then on, the Hodag's gone—
at least, not in your camp.
The years of labor trundle on, but still . . .
You know it watches.

ABOUT THE CRYPTIDS

A. P. HAWKINS is a sentient fungus in human form who would rather be moldering on the forest floor. We're not sure what she's using her sentience for, but we definitely heard her whispering to the plants in your garden last night. If only we could understand what she said.

ALEX BAUER is a northern-bred cryptid most at home in a good dark forest. He prefers communicating by inhuman chittering, but writing is a very close second.

ANGéLIQUE JAMAIL is a ninja-like cryptid: you don't notice how weird she is at first until it's too late and you're already ensorcelled. She can usually be found under a disco ball, mollifying her teaching assistant (a dog-like feline who lives on her desk) with New Wave music, and eating All The Chocolate. Proceed with caution, but definitely buy her books and take her classes. You know you want to.

ANNA GUENNADIEVNA is a swamp cryptid who's only ever spotted by cats and bookstore owners as she wanders the world on her trusty broomstick.

KT SETO has almost finished her Chesapeake Region Forest Crone certification exam and is really, really sorry about the plague.

NJ SULLIVAN is a soul-shaped hole forgotten by God. In his free time he enjoys barking at cows and complaining about the weather on Saturn's moon Titan. He is survived by a sentient thundercloud named Linda that followed him everywhere and a large collection of root beer bottles. He will not be missed, due to never having existed in the first place.

RUE SPARKS is the physical manifestation of all the discord and stubbornness within the fabric of existence, stuffed into a sack of bones and myofascial pain. According to the foremost specialists, their brain is too large for their skull and as such they will be undergoing neurosurgery in the fall. They cannot promise anything they create will make sense after that, either.

SARAH TOLLOK materializes into your home and spirits away the books you've allowed to languish in your TBR pile for far too long. In their place, she leaves vaguely insulting puns etched into mushroom caps, and the lingering scent of disappointment.

SIANYN LEIGH makes her nest in the wilds of central Illinois. Skittish around humans, she prefers the sanctity of the shadows and only ventures forth to forage for tasty snacks. It is said that on a quiet night, you can hear the haunting tunes of cult classic theme songs echoing over the rolling cornfields.

YNES FREEMAN is a southern cryptid who basks in cars that have been sitting all day in the summer sun. It is rumored that she bathes in lava.